AND SO WAS

ARABELLA.

SOME OF THE OTHER
PUPILS AT
THE
MAMMOTH
ACADEMY

← FLY LIVED IN
THE ACADEMY BUT
WASN'T A ~~PUIL~~ PUPIL.

CAVE
CAT

ORMSBY

OWL

PRUNELLA

FOX

A FEW MORE PUPILS OF THE MAMMOTH ACADEMY

REGINALD

RHONDA

REMI

ROGER

REX

RUFUS

REENIE

GIANT
GROUND
SLOTH

CAVE
BEAR

Some of the PUPILS OF THE...

PROFESSOR UGH

Professor
UGH teaches
THE PUPILS
OF the
CAVE
SKOOL

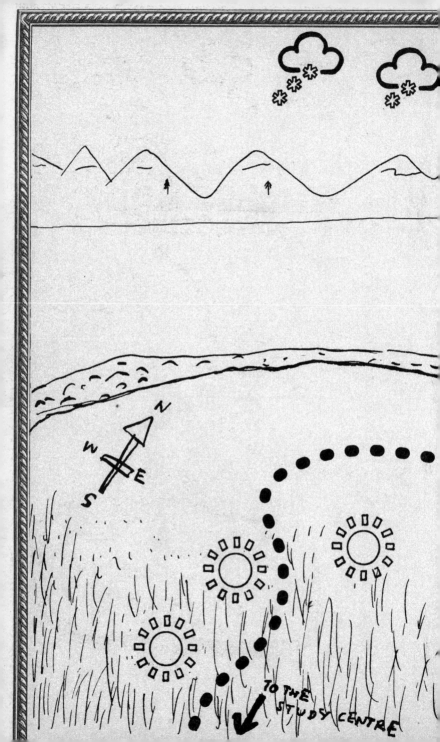

THE MAMMOTH ACADEMY
THE MARSHY MARSH
THE ALMOST IMPOSSIBLE TO CROSS GLACIER
A MAP OF THE MAMMOTH LANDS showing the route to THE PALMTREE SPRINGS STUDY CENTRE

For Tom and Toby, the Setchell boys

First published in Great Britain in 2008
by Hodder Children's Books

1

A Catalogue record for this book is available from the British Library

ISBN: 978 0 340 93031 1

Printed in the UK by CPI Bookmarque, Croydon, CR0 4TD

The paper and board used in this paperback by Hodder Children's Books
are natural recyclable products made from wood grown in sustainable forests.
The manufacturing processes conform to the environmental
regulations of the country of origin.

Hodder Children's Books
a division of Hachette Children's Books
338 Euston Road, London NW1 3BH
An Hachette Livre UK Company.

CHAPTER 1
THE STUDY TRIP

Oscar was a Woolly Mammoth, and so was Arabella. They were both pupils at the Mammoth Academy.

Normally they would spend their school days doing lessons in classrooms and writing things up in books, but this term was going to be different because this term the entire first year were going on a STUDY TRIP!

THIS VERY IMPORTANT LETTER ARRIVED BY MAMMOTH MAIL

Dear First Year,

The new term will begin very soon with a three week trip to
THE PALM TREE SPRINGS STUDY CENTRE.

Whilst you are there you will learn about the rare animals,
insects and plants of the region, and hopefully have lots of
fun too.

<u>A list of things needed for the trip</u>

A pair of sunglasses.
A swimming costume.
Suncream and a sun hat.
Binoculars or a telescope.
A towel.
Soap.
A tusk brush and tusk paste.
A sleeping bag.
Lots of pencils.
And some notebooks to make notes in.

All students will meet at 9.00am on the first day and leave
shortly after, returning at 5pm three weeks later.

Signed

Professor Snort

← THIS LEAFLET WAS ATTACHED TO THE LETTER...

The Palm Tree Springs Study Centre

Have a relaxing time and learn things at **The Palm Tree Springs Study Centre**. Enjoy a warm welcome from the proprietor Jimmy Giant Sloth.

Spend lazy afternoons relaxing by the beautiful river.

Enjoy walks along the riverside paths and view the remarkable animals of the region close up in the Centre's own HIDE.

Delicious meals will be made by our wonderful cook Jenny Giant Sloth.

We hope you enjoy your stay.

Thank you,

Jimmy and Jenny
Giant Sloth

Oscar and Arabella were looking forward to it because they had never been on a study trip before.

Fox was looking forward to it because it would give him a chance to try out his snorkel and flippers. Prunella was looking forward to it because it would give her a chance to work on her tan.

And Ormsby was looking forward to it because it would give him a chance to try his brand new CAMERA that he said was much more useful and interesting than a snorkel and flippers anyday.

So as you can see everyone was looking forward to it for one reason or another because everybody enjoys going on holiday.

On the first day back, as they walked to the meeting place outside the Academy, they greeted the friendly megaloceros and crossed the almost impossible to cross glacier. Everyone was in high spirits carrying backpacks, panniers and suitcases packed full of holiday things.

24

Fox was showing his snorkel to Oscar and
Arabella…

'So you see I'll be UNDER the water
LOOKING at all the fish and things and still able to
breathe!' said Fox, and Oscar seemed quite impressed.

Ormsby took a photo of Oscar looking impressed that he said made him look like a confused rat.

The rabbits seemed to think this was funny.

There was a big crowd of students and parents
gathered at the school gates. Everybody was making
lots of noise.

'What do you mean they have to WALK
hundreds of mammoth miles past the marshy marsh,
across the icy plains and through the grassy tundra to
get there?' said one mother. 'I'm not having my
Ormsby walk all that way!'

'It's good exercise and it should only take
eight or nine hours…' replied Professor Snout.

'Yay, this is going to be so much fun!'

'Now don't forget to write…'

'You have remembered your tusk brush dear haven't you…'

'And remember to wear your sunhat!'

And eventually once Giant Sloth had arrived (he was a bit late) it was time for them to set off. HONK! HONK! HONK!

'Hey, do you want a barley sugar?' said Fox.
'Sure thing,' said Oscar.
'I'll have one,' said Ormsby.
'Me too.'
'Thanks, Fox.'
'Don't mind if I do…'
'Mmmmmm!'

CHAPTER 2
ON THE ROAD

As they walked there was lots of excited chatter.
Ormsby was sure he had forgotten something.
Oscar said considering the size of Ormsby's
backpack that was impossible.

Ormsby was also sure that there must have
been an easier way to arrive, rather than walking
all the way, and he spent the next hour grumbling
about it.

All the time their route was travelling south, following the edge of the marshy marsh, heading towards the icy plains.

None of them had ever travelled that far from the Academy before. It was very exciting.

HONK

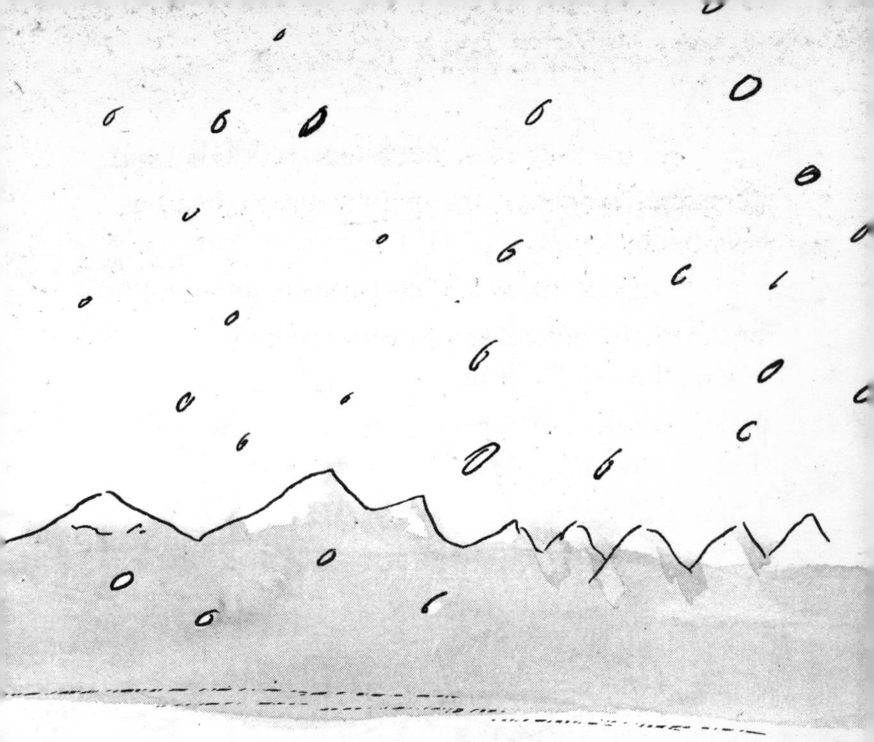

Gradually the scenery became less icy and more grassy. The sun had also started to become a little hotter so HONK! HONK! the call went out from Professor Snout for all the students to put on their sunhats and sunglasses. It was at this point that one of the rabbits realized he had forgotten his rucksack, which had everything in it including his sunhat and sunglasses.

'Well, there's nothing we can do about it now,'
said Professor Snout. 'You'll just have to make do.
Ormsby seems to have spares of everything in his
pack. You can borrow his extra sunhat and
sunglasses…'

The afternoon's travel became much less interesting than the morning's. It just seemed to be grass wherever you looked. Grass, grass and yet more grass.

Oscar suggested they play a game of 'I spy' to help pass the time.

'I spy with my mammoth eye some thing beginning with g.'

'Could it be *grass*?' said Ormsby.

More hours passed and many more miles
were trodden.

They had grass sandwiches for lunch.
And grass sandwiches for tea.

And so they continued…

'Are we there yet?' asked one of the rabbits.

'No, we're not,' said Professor Snout. He seemed to be becoming a little short-tempered. It was much hotter now and his sweaty brow and trunk had caused the map to get a little damp.

Ten minutes later another one of the rabbits asked, 'Are we there yet?'

'No, I'm afraid we are not there yet.'

And then a couple of minutes later Ormsby asked, 'Are we there yet?'

'NO ORMSBY. WE ARE NOT THERE YET.'

Ormsby sniggered.

Their progress became slower and slower as everyone succumbed to the heat. They also had to keep stopping to let Ormsby catch up, which made them even slower.

In fact, the only member of the party who wasn't having difficulties with the hot weather was Giant Sloth. He had started out at the rear of the group but now he was right at the front.

'Come on guys, hurry up!'

Oscar had never seen him so lively before.

'I guess he likes the heat,' said Arabella.

As the afternoon progressed it began to get even hotter, and everyone began to get even slower. Giant Sloth was still at the front of the group, despite offering to help carry everyone's bags.

'Come on, we'll never get there at this rate!'

And as the sun began to set everyone began to look very tired indeed.

'Are we there yet?' croaked Ormsby but nobody replied.

Eventually they heard Giant Sloth cry out from the darkness ahead, 'It's there, I can see it – THE PALM TREE SPRINGS STUDY CENTRE!'

CHAPTER 3
THE PALM TREE SPRINGS STUDY CENTRE

'Hello?'

   'HELLLOO?!'

   'ANYONE HERE?!'

   'HELLO?!'

   'MR JIMMY GIANT SLOTH?'

'It's all locked up.'

'What do we do?'

'Well, they must not have expected us to arrive so late,' said Professor Snout. 'Perhaps there's a key under the doormat?'

THE PALM TREE SPRINGS STUDY CENTRE

But there wasn't a doormat, or a key to be found anywhere.

Then Arabella noticed an open window at the top of the building and with Giant Sloth and Oscar's help they managed to get Prunella (the smallest animal in the Mammoth Academy) through it and inside.

A few moments later she had found her way downstairs and opened the front door.

'It seems to be completely deserted,' she said.

'So much for the friendly welcome,' muttered Ormsby.

'Well, as I say,' said Professor Snout, 'Mr Jimmy Giant Sloth probably didn't expect us to arrive so late and he left early.'

'Right, in you go everyone and let's see if we can get the rest of the lights working.'

Everything was covered in sheets thick with dust and cobwebs.

'Yuck!' said Ormsby. 'My mother would never stand for this in our home.'

Giant Sloth started removing the dustsheets and let out an enormous SNEEZE. Ormsby captured the moment with his new camera.

'This accommodation is unacceptable. It hasn't been cleaned in months!'

'Right, students,' interrupted Professor Snout. 'I'm sorry about the welcome and the slightly dusty accommodation. I'm sure it will all be better once we meet Mr Jimmy Giant Sloth and Mrs Jenny Giant Sloth in the morning. Here are the keys to your rooms. I suggest you all bed down and get a good night's rest — we've got a busy day's study ahead of us tomorrow.'

The rooms weren't as clean and cosy as those shown in the brochure. They were full of dust, cobwebs and INSECTS.

Ormsby said he was going to squash them all with his foot but Giant Sloth said that they weren't harmful, and that they were rare *Spiderpedes* that only lived in the Palm Tree Springs area, and that they had more right to be there than them because the Spiderpedes were there first.

And so everyone began to make themselves as comfortable as possible and tried to get to sleep.

Professor popped his head in to make sure everyone was OK, turned the light off and closed the door, looking tired and slightly worried.

CHAPTER 4
THE PLOT THICKENS

The next morning all the students awoke really early with the sun shining into their rooms. It was only seven o'clock but it was already very hot.

'Wakey wakey!' called Giant Sloth.

And everyone began shambling their way

down to the dining room for breakfast.

Except there wasn't any breakfast…

Or any sign of Jenny Giant Sloth the cook, or Jimmy Giant Sloth the hotelier.

Oscar thought Professor Snout was beginning to look a little bit more worried and tired. It didn't look like he'd slept well at all.

Giant Sloth sped towards the kitchen.

'Don't worry folks, I'll sort us out some food to eat.'

And after much opening and shutting of cupboards he began frying and sizzling.

'It's an old giant sloth speciality dish of the region, and one of my favourite meals,' he said.

'There is NO WAY I'm going to eat THAT for breakfast,' said Ormsby as he took yet another photo to show his mother. 'I'm off to find a café and get some real food.'

Outside the Study Centre was even hotter than inside the Study Centre. As Ormsby's eyes grew accustomed to the brilliant sunlight he scanned the horizon for a café, ice cream parlour or even a newspaper shop, but saw nothing. Just leafy palm trees, enormous tropical plants and a strange pair of eyes looking back at him.

Ormsby stared in shock as the eyes fluttered their long eyelashes and he heard a whinnying-giggling sound.

'Heh heh heh heheheheh.'

He decided to beat a hasty retreat back into the Study Centre's dining room to find what was left of the fried bat, tinned squid and cactus...

'Right, there you are, Ormsby,' said Professor Snout. 'I do wish you wouldn't go wandering off like that. Now, it would seem that the proprietor has made some mistake about our booking, so we will continue with our planned study day and hopefully by the time we get back he will have returned.'

And he began handing out the study sheets.

DAY ONE STUDY SHEET

Today we will study the river and the
riverside and see what plants and
animals live there.

Then we will walk to THE HIDE.

'Great, I can use my snorkel and flippers and see what's living IN it!' said Fox.

And before anyone could do or say anything Fox had grabbed his snorkel, flippers and swimming costume and jumped from the top of the roof down into the water.

'Glug. Can't see much. Glug there's lots of things bobbing about. No fishes though…glug.'

'Euch! I think you'd better take a shower, Fox!'
said Giant Sloth.

'There is no way I'm swimming in THAT,'
said Ormsby as he snapped a picture of Fox
emerging from the stinking water.

'My mother is going to hear about this as well,' he said.

'It's not like it looked in the catalogue,' said Arabella.

'It smells,' said Oscar.

'Yes, it is rather whiffy,' said Professor Snout. 'I think perhaps the rest of us might want to miss out on a swim,' he continued, folding his towel away. 'Make sure you make a note of this on the worksheet and then we'll set off exploring further along the river bank towards THE HIDE...'

WORKSHEET 1A)

THE RIVER

Number of fish ~~None~~ NONE

Other animals FLIES

Freshness of the water STINKY

Number of feeding animals NONE

We also saw LOTS OF THINGS BOBBING ABOUT

The students set off with Giant Sloth at the front of the group telling everyone about the different plants. Oscar and Arabella had never seen him so talkative before.

'And this is a Spinytaculus plant. It's very prickly so be careful…

'And this is a Hoff Flower… I haven't seen one of these since I was a small boy… I grew up around here you see… it doesn't look very healthy though…'

Ormsby was at the back of the group. He was having a grumble about the smell of the river, the smell of Fox and lots of other things, when suddenly he heard a whinnying sound behind him and there hiding amongst the leaves and flowers were the eyes again.

The eyes fluttered their eyelids and Ormsby heard the same whinnying noise.

'Heh heh heh heheheheh giggle.'

Ormsby spun round and made his way to the front of the group as fast as he could.

CHAPTER 5
THE HIDE

The riverside walk wasn't as described in the holiday brochure either.

WORKSHEET 1B)

THE RIVERSIDE WALK

Number of plants Some but not very healthy looking.

Number of feeding animals None.

Other Notes More flies and stinky smells and things floating downstream in the smelly river.

The group trudged on, following the path beside the river as it wove through the undergrowth. Eventually they arrived at the hide.

'Right, here we are. Now, Palm Tree Springs is one of the best places to see Glyptodonts in the whole world,' began Professor Snout.

'Here is a sheet telling you all about them…'

GLYPTODONTS

Glyptodonts are creatures unlike any others. They are about 1.5 metres tall and heavily armoured.

Despite their appearance they are very shy.

They like to live by the water's edge.

They are vegetarians.

Some Glyptodonts feeding by the water's edge.

SCALY ARMOUR PLATING

SPIKY TAIL

Picture of a Glyptodont showing its scaly armour-plating and spiky tail.

'THE HIDE has been set up so we can view the Glyptodonts feeding without disturbing them, but it is only big enough for two or three at a time so I'd like the rest of you to sit outside and patiently wait your turn.

'There will be another worksheet for you to fill in inside the hide.'

THIS IS
ORMSBY'S
WORKSHEET

WORKSHEET 2A)

IN THE HIDE

Number of Glyptodonts in 1 hour **0**

Number of Glyptodonts in 2 hours **0**

Number of Glyptodonts in 3 hours **0**

Activities of the Glyptodonts ~~NOTHING~~

BECAUSE WE
DIDNT SEE
ANY

'What a waste of time!' said Ormsby. 'This study trip is rubbish. The brochure showed Glyptodonts everywhere, but we haven't seen ANY wild animals AT ALL. This place is a dump. Well, I've had enough. I'm going back to the Study Centre to phone my mother and tell her all about it…'

Ormsby hadn't gone far before he stopped dead in his tracks.

It was the eyes again.

The eyes looked at Ormsby and Ormsby looked back at the eyes.

They fluttered their long eyelashes and he heard the familiar giggling.

This went on for quite some time until suddenly they were gone and Ormsby began to hear very different, much more aggressive noises, coming from another part of the forest.

UGH! UGH! UGH!

CHAPTER 6
KOSTA UGH

'Do you think it's wise for Ormsby to be on his own?' said Arabella. 'I mean, what happens if he gets lost or something?'

'At least we might get some peace and quiet,' said Oscar.

'I'll go and see where he's gone,' said Giant Sloth. 'I'm feeling like a quick stroll anyway.'

Giant Sloth hadn't strolled far before he heard some very loud aggressive noises coming from up ahead.

UGH! UGH! UGH!

And peering through the leaves he could see about twenty HUMANS walking towards him, armed with clubs and spears…!

He spun round and began running back towards the others.

'QUIIIIICK!' he said as he burst into view. 'HUMANS!

'Coming this way armed with spears and clubs!'
'EVERYONE INTO THE HIDE!' shouted
Arabella.

Inside the hide all the students held their breath as the group of humans came into view. They had been taught all about humans in their lessons back at the Academy.

There was one adult and twelve or thirteen cubs. They looked quite hot and angry. The small humans were running around and the adult human kept shouting at them.

'Now I want all of you to remain very very quiet,' whispered Professor Snout under his breath. 'If those humans see or hear us they will try and attack us and eat us!'

And very carefully he found his binoculars and put them up to his eyes. When the rest of the mammoths saw this, they did the same.

'Remarkable...'

The humans didn't seem to have noticed the hide, and carried on grunting and hitting each other, completely unaware they were being watched.

And the group picked up their clubs and other things and began walking down the path in the opposite direction…

...followed by the HIDE.

The path twisted and turned through the undergrowth. Every time the humans stopped, the HIDE stopped too.

The humans seemed to be getting more and more excited until they rounded a corner and this is what they saw…

There were stalls selling glypto burgers, iced eels and 'KOSTA UGH' hats.

The adult humans were laid out on the sand asleep whilst the younger cubs ran about making loads of noise screaming, jumping and splashing in the water.

Over to one side a small group of humans were hitting drums with bones and making a REALLY LOUD repetitive monotonous beat.

BOOM-BOOM, BOOM-BOOM-BOOM.

BOOM-BOOM, BOOM-BOOM-BOOM.

BOOM-BOOM, BOOM-BOOM-BOOM.

Other humans of all ages seemed to be dancing to it.

There was also a little sign that said, 'Cave skool is shut coz we is on holiday'.

There was rubbish everywhere. And lots of makeshift huts and sun umbrellas made from felled palm trees.

Then one of the humans got up, went to the toilet in the water, and then flopped back down again into the sand. Another human finished an ice cream and threw the wrapper into the water.

Inside the hide the mammoths began whispering to one another…

CHAPTER 7
MISSING!

'OK. When was the last time anyone saw Ormsby?' asked Professor Snout.

Everyone shook their heads.

'It was just before the humans came,' said Arabella. 'Ormsby left on his own to go back to the Study Centre.'

'He must have been captured by the humans. Oh dear, this is very bad, very bad indeed. What will his mother say?'

Professor Snout began to look very worried.

'Perhaps we can rescue him…' said Arabella.

Professor Snout thought about this for a moment.

ORMSBY'S MUM ←

'Right, everyone get their binoculars and
telescopes ready for spotting Orsmby extra-specially
quickly. We're going on a rescue mission!'

Meanwhile, Giant Sloth made a few preparations of his own…

And very carefully the mammoths in THE
HIDE began to walk about, peering into each hut
and under each sun umbrella for a sign of Ormsby.
Wherever they went, Giant Sloth would leave a sign,
or a litter bin, or even a handy toilet.

It was slow, hot work and so far not a trace of
Ormsby was to be found anywhere…

103

Whether it was the extremely hot day that
started it, or some disagreement over a towel beside
the lake, or Giant Sloth's helpful notes, nobody knew,
but the humans had become very agitated.

Posters were being ripped down and thrown
into the water.

Beach beds were thrown into the water.

More palm trees were ripped down and thrown into the water.

Even the toilet that the Giant Sloth had made for them was torn apart and thrown in the water.

Inside THE HIDE the mammoths began to get very worried.

'I think they've seen us!'

BUT…

All the rubbish being so carelessly thrown away was causing another problem downstream. A BIG problem…

The debris had completely blocked the river and KOSTA UGH was beginning to flood!

CHAPTER 8
FLOOD!

Within minutes the beach was covered in whirling water, then the tree roots, and the tree trunks until even the tops of some of the trees were completely submerged.

Very soon the humans' feet were swept from underneath them and they began to bob about in the swirling river.

Inside THE HIDE the mammoths were panicking.

'I can't open the door,' said Prunella. 'It's jammed up with rubbish.'

The water level had by now reached the viewing flaps.

'Keep walking towards higher ground,' shouted Professor Snout.

But the waters kept rising. There was no way they could make it in time.

Suddenly Fox shouted, 'QUICK, I've just had an idea! Right, close all the viewing panels and give me your telescopes and binoculars.'

'Now, everyone who has a trunk raise it up like a snorkel and start getting air from the surface.

'Up periscope!

'And I'll hang my flippers out the back to paddle us to safety.'

FOX'S PERISCOPE

FOX'S FLIPPERS

And soon the mammoths found themselves safely huddled on top of a tall rock.

The humans hadn't been quite so fortunate though. The whirling waters had torn up all their KOSTA UGH buildings and they were bobbing about amongst all the rubbish.

UGH! UGH!

'I wonder what's going to happen next?' said Oscar.

The water continued rising higher and higher until suddenly downstream the dam burst.

'It's just like someone flushing a toilet,' remarked Giant Sloth as everything whirled round and round and round before disappearing downstream through rapids, over waterfalls and far out to sea.

'Crumbs,' said one mammoth.

The flood waters had completely washed away all trace of KOSTA UGH and the humans. All that was left were a few bedraggled plants.

And then everyone remembered Ormsby. 'Poor Ormsby,' they all said.

'He must have been eaten by the humans…'

'Or drowned in the flood…'

'I really will miss the old chap…'

'Even if he was really annoying at times.'

'Hello. Did someone mention my name?'

And there, a little higher up the hillside, was Ormsby, sitting beside an enormous Glyptodont with big fluttering eyelashes.

'ORMSBY! THERE YOU ARE!'

'Hello, Professor Snout, how are you?' Ormsby shouted back. 'This is Gladice, she's a Glyptodont. Hasn't she got the most wonderful eyes?'

Ormsby blushed and Gladice giggled and fluttered her eyelids.

Professor Snout stood speechless.

'Gladice took me to see the other Glyptodonts that are hiding up in the mountains. Apparently there are some humans about… so be careful…

'And here's Jimmy and Jenny Giant Sloth. They've been hiding in the mountains too. Terribly nice people. Jenny is a terrific cook you know.

'Have I missed anything?'

At this point Professor Snout went bright purple and was unable to say ANYTHING except, 'I   n e e d   a   h o l i d a y...'

CHAPTER 9
BONNES VACANCES

With everyone helping, it didn't take too long to clear up. The water had completely washed away all the humans and their rubbish, and all the water and mud had actually helped some of the plants to grow back again.

The Glyptodonts came back to feed. (They didn't seem to mind the mammoths at all.) And fish started to appear back in the river.

Gradually Palm Tree Springs began to look like the beautiful place it was before the humans arrived.

After that, Professor Snout said it was too hot to do any more schoolwork and that the rest of the trip would be spent relaxing on the beach!

'Hurray!'

So whilst Professor Snout sat in the shade and quietly wrote up his notes about the close encounter with humans:

Oscar and Fox did lots of snorkelling.

Prunella and Arabella worked on their tans and had nice chats with Gladice. (Whilst Ormsby sat quietly beside and looked longingly into her eyes. 'Ahhhhhhh.')

Jimmy and Jenny Giant Sloth set up a stall serving ice creams and ice lollies – with Giant Sloth helping to run it.

And everyone had a thoroughly enjoyable time.

Before they knew it, three weeks had passed and it was time to go home.

There were lots of goodbyes.

Giant Sloth said goodbye to Jimmy and Jenny Giant Sloth. Ormsby bade a teary farewell to Gladice. Everyone waved goodbye to the PALM TREE SPRINGS STUDY CENTRE.

And it was time to leave.

CHAPTER 10
WELCOME HOME

The walk back to the Mammoth Academy seemed to go much quicker than the journey there, mainly because there was so much to talk about…

And then many hours later, with sore feet and dusty trunks, the weary mammoths made it across the grassy plains, over the icy wastes, back to the Mammoth Academy gates, to be greeted by everyone.

Whilst Cook prepared the special dinner, they told stories of their amazing trip.

The head mistress agreed that all the students had done extra-specially well in saving the nature resort of Palm Tree Springs. She also seemed very interested in Professor Snout's human study.

Ormsby was the only one who was quiet. He just sat there looking at a crumpled photo of Gladice.

'But did you have a good time?' said his mother. 'Was the accommodation acceptable?'

SIGH...

And then with a fanfare of mammoth trunks,
Cook appeared from the kitchen with her special
welcome home dinner of…

'Fried bat, tinned squid and cactus. A regional speciality from Palm Tree Springs, and something to remind you of your holiday…'

'FRIED BAT, SQUID AND CACTUS?' said Giant Sloth. 'YUM! My favourite!!'

Another mammoth adventure from Smarties Award winner Neal Layton

MAMMOTH ACADEMY

Q. What's the difference between a Woolly Mammoth and a gooseberry?

A. Woolly Mammoths don't grow on bushes

Oscar was a Woolly Mammoth, and so was Arabella. They lived a long time ago in the Ice Age...

Oscar and Fox have heard all about HUMANS – horrible hairless beings with big bashing clubs. And one day while out on a BIG ADVENTURE, they finally learn the most important lesson in Mammothdom –

HOW TO SURVIVE!

BEWARE HUMANS!!

'This book gets 10/10...'
Professor Snout

'As funny as ever with quirky and delightful illustrations.'
Betty Bookmark

Another mammoth adventure from Smarties Award winner Neal Layton

MAMMOTH ACADEMY
IN TROUBLE

Oscar was a Woolly Mammoth, and so was Arabella. They lived a long time ago in the Ice Age…

There is graffiti on the wall of the Academy. It can only mean one thing – HUMANS!

And then the scratching begins… FLEAS!

Luckily Arabella and her best friend Prunella have been concentrating in class. And the results are quite simply explosive!

**'Goes off with a bang!'
Professor Snout**

Another tale from Smarties Award winner
Neal Layton

THE STORY OF EVERYTHING

BY NEAL LAYTON

Once upon a very long time ago there was nothing.

No space, no time, no planets, no people, no me, no you, no nothing, until...

An ingenious novelty book about evolution.
It will literally BLOW YOU AWAY!